Trafalgar Tr,

Written by: Stephen Cosgrove
Illustrated by: Robin James

A Serendipity Book

PRICE/STERN/SLOAN
Publishers, Inc., Los Angeles
1980

Dedicated to Larry Sloan, my friend and inspiration for Trafalgar True.

Stephen

Far, far away, in a time of dreams and make-believe there was a small curious country called Kurium.

Kurium wasn't much as countries go: a small forest, a medium-sized meadow, and a twisting crystal stream. What made Kurium very special was that right in the middle of the meadow lived a most magnificent, winged dragon called Trafalgar True.

Trafalgar didn't do much from one day to the next. He would sit and quietly watch the world go 'round, Trafalgar loved every living thing and watching, to him, was the same as doing.

Trafalgar would watch the flock of birds as they flew from tree to tree. He would watch a turtle or two as they crawled across the meadow. But most of all, he loved to watch the furry little creatures called Kith and Kin.

There was very little difference between a Kith and a Kin. They both had long bushy tails and big brown eyes. In fact, the only difference was that Kith's fur was black with a long, white stripe down the middle, while the Kin's fur was white with a black stripe down the middle.

All day, every day, they would skitter about the forest playing games with one another in the happiest of ways, filling Trafalgar with love for them all.

Everyone would have been happy to this very day if, early one morning, a piece of the sun had not fallen from the sky and landed right in the middle of Trafalgar's meadow.

When the dust had settled, Trafalgar saw the most beautiful Sunstone he had ever seen. The morning light danced and glittered from the stone, making everthing seem a little brighter.

It couldn't have been more than a moment or two before all the Kith and Kin had gathered around to gaze at the Sunstone's beauty. They were "oohhing" and "aahhing" at its brilliance when either a Kith or a Kin pushed someone else to get just a little closer. Soon, Kith were pushing Kin and Kin were pushing Kith.

"Quit your pushing!" snarled a fuzzy little Kin. "Just stand back! In a minute I'll let you see my stone."

"Your stone!" growled the Kith. "It landed on our side of the forest. The stone belongs to the Kith!"

And so it went throughout the day with the Kin grumbling, the Kith pushing, and Trafalgar watching in disbelief.

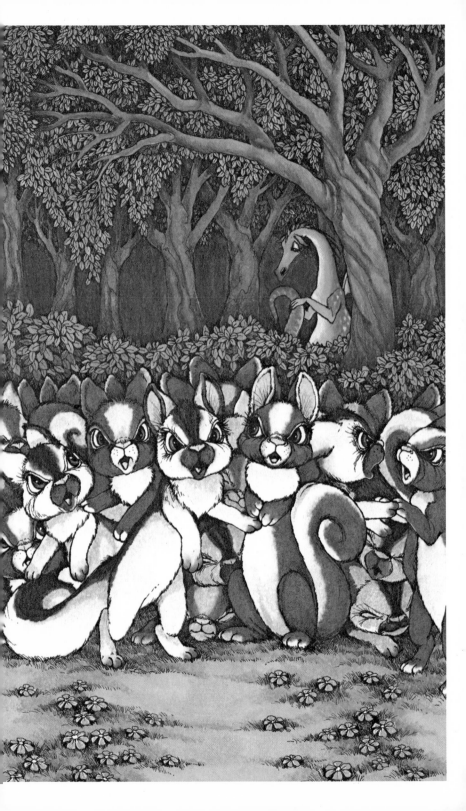

The next day was the same — if not a little worse — as the Kith and Kin tossed insult after insult at one another. Why, one poor Kith was even tripped as he walked down the path. As he picked himself up he could hear laughter coming from the bushes around him.

"Dumb old Kith," giggled the hidden Kin. "They think the Sunstone belongs to them when we all know it belongs to us!" Then laughing and chuckling, off they scampered back to the meadow.

Trafalgar True sat and watched, unnoticed. Where before there was a pleasant little meadow filled with love, there was now nothing but a field of bitterness and jealousy. So saddened was he by this turn of events that large silver tears began to glide gracefully over his snoot and fall softly to the ground.

It wasn't that the Kith hated the Kin or that the Kin hated the Kith, it was just that each wanted to own the brilliance of the Sunstone and neither knew how to share. All day long there was pushing and shoving as they tried to be closest to the brilliant stone.

The Kith became so frustrated that later that very same day they threw a vine over the stone and tried to drag it away. The Kin, not to be outdone, threw a vine from the other side and the two silly groups pulled and tugged for nearly three hours before they all collapsed, too pooped to pop.

In fact, they were so tired from all that pushing and pulling that they fell fast asleep right there in the meadow. All, that is, save for a baby Kin who stood before the stone and softly cried, "I hate you, Sunstone. You're so pretty but all you have brought is sadness. I wish you would go back to the sun!"

No one heard the child except the stone and a silent figure who watched from beneath a tree, Trafalgar True.

A saddened and troubled Trafalgar thought and thought throughout the night. Just before dawn he knew what he had to do. He quietly flexed his wings once or twice, then gently flew to the magnificent stone. With all his might he clutched the Sunstone firmly in his arms and began to fly towards the sun as the morning light was just breaking through the trees.

The morning air was filled with soft sighs as the Kith and Kin woke from their sleep and gently rubbed their eyes.

Suddenly someone shouted, "It's gone! The Kith stole the Sunstone!" "No," cried the Kith, "it was the Kin!"

With that they began shoving and shouting and a Kin even pulled a Kith's tail. There would have been a terrible fight if it had not been for someone who looked up and saw Trafalgar high in the sky.

"Look! It's Trafalgar True and he's got the stone!"

"Oh, no!" cried the baby Kin. "Trafalgar is trying to fly the stone back to the sun!"

As the Kith and Kin gazed into the sky they realized what they had done.

"But he'll be killed!" they moaned. "We've got to stop him!"

They all looked at one another, trying desperately to think of a way to reach Trafalgar.

Suddenly, one furry Kith snapped his fingers and said, "I know. We must all shout together. With all of our voices united he will surely hear us."

Together they formed a circle and while holding hands began to shout, "Trafalgar! Trafalgar!"

For a moment it looked as though the plan was going to fail but then, Trafalgar heard the echo of his name. He slowly turned in the sky and looked down on the creatures below.

"You cannot fly to the sun. For if you do, you will surely die!" they cried. "Our selfishness and greed has almost destroyed you as well as our friendship. Please, come back."

Trafalgar smiled softly and then began to glide gently back to the land of Kurium.

From that time forward Kith and Kin shared and shared alike in the meadows of Kurium. They would play around the Sunstone in the happiest of ways, filling Trafalgar with love for them all.

So, when it comes to sharing
With Kith and Kin or you,
Remember what you're sharing
Is the love of Trafalgar True.

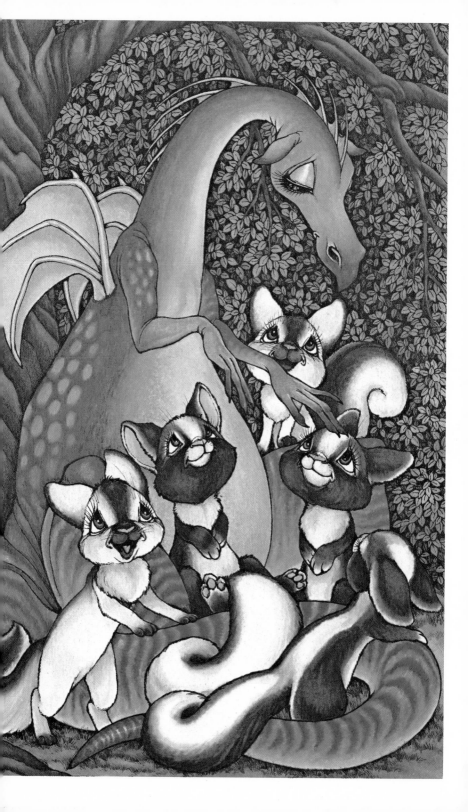

Serendipity Books

Written by
Stephen Cosgrove

Illustrated by
Robin James

In Search of the Saveopotomas
The Muffin Muncher
Serendipity
Jake O'Shawnasey
Morgan and Me
Flutterby
Nitter Pitter
Leo The Lop
Leo The Lop-Tail Two
Leo The Lop-Tail Three
Snaffles
Kartusch

The Gnome From Nome
The Wheedle on the Needle
The Dream Tree
Hucklebug
Creole
Bangalee
Catundra
Cap'n Smudge
Maui-Maui
Little Mouse on the Prairie
Shimmeree
Trafalgar True

$1.50 each

Boxed Sets Nos. 1, 2, 3, 4
(5 books in each set) $7.50 per set

Serendipity Books are available wherever books are sold
or may be obtained from the publisher by sending price of book
or boxed set, plus 50 cents for handling and mailing.

PRICE/STERN/SLOAN *Publishers, Inc.*
410 North La Cienega Boulevard, Los Angeles, California 90048